Rudolf Buddensieg

John Wiclif

Patriot and Reformer

Rudolf Buddensieg

John Wiclif
Patriot and Reformer

ISBN/EAN: 9783337307448

Printed in Europe, USA, Canada, Australia, Japan

Cover: Foto ©Raphael Reischuk / pixelio.de

More available books at www.hansebooks.com

··I troBe that in the ende the truth
Bill conquere.··

John Wiclif

PATRIOT & REFORMER

Life and Writings
of
RUDOLF BUDDENSIEG
LIC. THEOL. LEIPSIC.

Quincentenary Edition

London
T. FISHER UNWIN
26 PATERNOSTER SQUARE
MDCCCLXXXIV.

CONTENTS.

PAGE

Contents.

PREFACE.

HE present little volume merely seeks — on the Quincentenary of John Wiclif's death—to recall to the memory of England one of her greatest sons, and to press home the thought of how much she owes to the advocate of her political and religious freedom, the translation of her Bible, or and the maker of her language. Designed for wide circulation and popular

1 *

use, it does not affect originality or new research as to the Reformer's life and doctrine. It is based on the works of Lechler, Shirley, Vaughan, Burrows, and Matthew, and on the Introduction to Wiclif's Polemical Works, issued last year by the present editor.

RUDOLF BUDDENSIEG.

BOOK I.

JOHN WICLIF.

HERE is in the University
Library of Prague a mag-
nificent old Bohemian
Cantionale written in the
year 1572, and adorned
with a number of finely illuminated
miniatures. One of the most characteristic of these little works of art stands
above a hymn in memory of John Hus,
the Reformer. It consists of three me-
dallions rising one above another, in the

first of which John Wiclif, the Englishman, is represented striking sparks out
of a stone. In the second, Hus, the
Bohemian, is setting fire to the coals;
while in the third, Luther, the German,
is bearing the fierce light of a blazing
torch.

The trilogy of these miniatures is a
fine illustration of the Divine mission
of the three great Reformers.

John Wiclif, the Englishman, is the
true, original spirit, the bringer of a
new light, another Prometheus in the
realm of spiritual things. Modern research at least testifies in a singular
manner to the truth of the miniature,
and is bringing about a great change
of opinion. Quite recently it has been
shown by a German writer that the
whole Bohemian movement of the
fifteenth century was simply an imita-
tion of the movement that had stirred
England—and more particularly Oxford
—under the influence of John Wiclif
thirty years before. It has been proved

conclusively that, as far as doctrine is concerned, Hus borrowed nearly all his reforming ideas from the strong-minded Yorkshireman. | In the works of the Oxford professor a rich fountain of new thought had been opened to him, by means of which he became the national and religious leader of a great people, the martyr of a great cause. The whole Husite movement ⁄ is mere Wiclifism. It should, therefore, never be forgotten, at least by English-men, that those mighty ideas which at one time seemed to strike the death blow to the Church of Rome, and made a whole empire tremble before their spiritual supremacy, did not originate with a Czech, but had an Englishman for their parent.

But it was not only by the generations following Wiclif that his overpowering influence was felt. He was also the first who, at a period of general help-lessness, when the Church, lost in world-liness, was unable to satisfy the spiritual

and national aspirations of her adhe-
rents, gave utterance to new ideas which
seemed fully to replace the fading tra-
ditional forms of life and thought ; and
who thus made England to become the
glorious leader of the greatest spiritual
movement of modern times—the Reformation of the Western branch of the
Catholic Church.

He it was who first dared to face the
system of corruption and tyranny which
had overspread all Europe, who first
showed in his own person how much
could be done against a whole world of
foes by one single-hearted man, who
had made himself the champion of
truth.

At the same time it was he who
brought a thorough change over medi-
eval Christianity by sweeping away
through his influence all its peculiar
forms of life and teaching—pardons,
indulgences, the merits of Saints, pilgrimages, images, and absolutions. He
was the first who denied transubstanti-

ation in the Holy Eucharist; he rejected
the doctrine of purgatory and the alleged
infallibility of the Church of Rome.
He proved the sufficiency of Holy
Scripture, rejected the claims of tra-
dition as opposed to Biblical teaching, and opened to his countrymen,
learned and simple, the fountain of a
new spiritual life by translating the
Bible for the first time into their
mother tongue.

England owes to him her Bible, her
present language, the reformation of the
Church, her religious and, to a very large
degree, her political liberty. He is not
only the acknowledged father of her
prose, his claims to our thankfulness
and admiration are greater; and the
more we learn of him, the more painful
does it appear that his most important
works should have been until now allowed to lie buried in manuscript.[1]

[1] Two volumes have recently been published,
as a first instalment, by the Wyclif Society,
containing the Polemical Works, and others
will follow in due course, as funds permit.

Dean Hook said, " John Wiclif may be justly accounted one of the greatest men that our country has produced. He is one of the very few who have left the impress of their minds not only on their own age but on all time." With Chaucer, Shakspere, and Milton he is one of the makers of the English language, and his influence in English religious life is unparalleled by any later man. He must, therefore, be pronounced to be the first, and by far the greatest, Reformer preceding the 16th century.

Great as was this leader of a new intellectual life, he is not so well known or understood by the present generation as he should be. England in particular has been ungrateful to his memory, and seems to have forgotten the claims to which he is justly entitled as the defender of her national liberties, the reformer of her religious life, and the translator of her Bible. So it comes to pass that his image looks down on many of his countrymen without personality or individual expression—as the dim portrait of a man half forgotten, though his spiritual influence had once been felt to a remarkable degree by the nation for more than a century.

We should, therefore, not allow the Quincentenary of his death to pass without bringing before our minds the personal history and the far-reaching influence of one in whom the characteristics of the Englishman and the Christian are united in like manner as those of the German and the Christian in Luther.

I.

Strangely enough, we find that the place and the date of the Reformer's birth are alike unknown. What little we know of either we owe to the old antiquarians and chroniclers of the 16th century. Leland says that Wiclif "drew his origin" from the little Yorkshire village of Wycliffe, situated on the banks of the Tees. He belonged to the old Wiclif family, which since the Norman Conquest had held the manor of the place and the patronage of its cure. Whether he was *born* there is still doubtful, and no remark of his own has yet been found in his works that throws any light upon the question.

There is also no certain date fixed for his birth as yet. In all probability the date given by Leland—A.D. 1324 —is wrong, and the real date is most likely a few years later—somewhere about A.D. 1330. Of his earlier years there is likewise nothing known. When fifteen years of age—as was usual at that time—he entered the University of Oxford, then at the height of its fame. Here for nearly a century the foremost men of intellect in Europe—Grosseteste, Roger Bacon, Duns Scotus, Occam, Bradwardine, and Richard Armagh— had been working among, and lecturing to, crowds of students, the number of whom once rose to upwards of 30,000.

In this golden age of intellectual activity young Wiclif went through the
" Trivium "— grammar, rhetoric, and
logic—and the " Quadrivium "—arith-
metic, music, geometry, and astronomy
—and took in due course the usual degrees in philosophy and theology. After
having studied for some time in Balliol
College, he became (from 1354–1356)
an inmate of Merton, and after a time
its seneschal, until in 1361 the Master-
ship of Balliol was conferred upon him.

So prominent had his influence in
the University by this time become
that from this date we never lose sight
of him.

Shortly afterwards he resigned his
post, accepted the little cure of Fylingham, in Lincolnshire, and in 1365 was
offered in very friendly terms by Archbishop Islip the Wardenship of the
newly founded Canterbury Hall, which
was afterwards incorporated with Christ
Church. In him the Primate had dis-
covered "a man of learning and good

character," whose "previous fidelity, circumspection, and diligence fitted him exactly for the delicate position in the Hall," the constitution of which had just been altered by the founder in favour of the Seculars. Wiclif had scarcely entered upon his post when the Regulars (Dominican Friars) protested against the infringement of the old rules, and a year later, with the influence of the new Primate, himself a monk, on their side, they triumphed over the Warden; for notwithstanding an appeal to the Pope himself, he did not succeed in averting an unfavourable decision of the authorities. Three years later he gave up Fylingham, and accepted the rectory of Ludgershall, in Buckinghamshire, which, being much nearer to Oxford, enabled him to keep up his old connection with the University. In 1374 he was presented by the crown to the rectory of Lutterworth, in Leicestershire, which cure he held until his death ten years later. During

all this time, however, Oxford continued to be the scene of his personal
influence. A voluminous series of
works was written by him "while stay-
ing in the schools," and in the University Registers his name is frequently
met with in connection with Queen's,[1]
where he resided, in rented rooms, in
1363-5, 1374-5, and in 1380. The
attempts of his adversaries, who once
and again had seized the reins of
office in the University, to silence him
in his lecture-room, and to undermine
his influence among the students,
finally resulted in a failure, as is proved
by the facts and dates already cited.

---

[1] I must not omit to mention, with reference
to Queen's, that it is in the college bills that
Wiclif's name for the first time appears in an
official document. Eleven years later, in the
Royal mandate of July 26, 1374, nominating the
Commissioners of the Bruges embassy, it first
appears in a public and authoritative document: in both it is spelt *Wiclif*. In fact this
form should settle the much-disputed ortho-
graphical question of his name.

By his opposition to the Regulars in the Canterbury Hall affair the eyes of the national anti-Papal party in the University had been directed towards him. In a personal matter he had risen to destroy the influence of the monkish party, which, at a time when Oxford had taken the place of Paris, had become a real danger to the great national institution, and thus to the country. So it happened that this personal quarrel grew into an affair of national importance, and so far IT IS THE TRUE BEGINNING OF THE ENGLISH REFORMATION. The unflinching though unsuccessful opposition of Wiclif to the partisans of the existing Papal system had made him the advocate of national liberty, and had pushed him into the foreground to do battle with a foreign power that openly denied to Englishmen the privilege of their freedom : Wiclif had indeed become a public character.

In consequence of a new quarrel

with a monk, concerning the right of
the king to punish delinquent priests
by fining them, he had likewise won
the sympathy of Edward the Third.
This great and chivalrous monarch
had, after the shameful humiliation of
John Lackland, set before himself the
glorious aim of recovering the position
won for the English people by Edward
the First. After his wars with the
French King he had to fight a still
harder battle against the French Pope
in Avignon ; but by arousing a truly
national spirit he succeeded.

There had been continual quarrels
about the tribute to be paid by the
English King to the Papal Court.
Edward the Third, with a good Parliament assisting him, succeeded in check-
ing the system of the Papal Provisions,
i.e., the privilege of the Pope to bestow
rich English benefices, the "seigniories,"
on foreigners who never set foot in
England, especially the Cardinals of
the Papal Court, who never came

near their cures. How deeply this system was rooted may be inferred from the fact, that upwards of 20,000 marks of the whole English Church revenues had to be paid to ecclesiastics residing in Avignon. From contemporary writers we know that one French Cardinal was Dean of York, another Dean of Salisbury, a third Dean of Lincoln, three others Archdeacons of Canterbury, Durham, and Suffolk, and three others again Prebendaries of Thane, Massingdon, and York.

The first signs of a national awakening in 1350 had been followed in 1353 by "the noble statute Præmunire," which condemned "all who should plead in the Papal Court to forfeiture, outlawry, and imprisonment," and which had thus become "the foundation stone of religious liberty in England."

At last, when in 1365 Pope Urban demanded from the English King the

arrears of thirty-three years' annual
tribute (of 1000 marks) as a feudal
acknowledgment of Papal supremacy
in England and Ireland, Edward, who
had not for a moment thought of
bowing to these priestly encroachments,
submitted the question to the decision
of the Parliament of 1366.

This claim of the Pope it was that
brought forward the warden of Canterbury Hall as a writer on a great public
subject, and made him the champion
of national rights. The ability he had
displayed in former University dis-
cussions had recommended him to the
favour of the King, who by this time
had conferred upon him the dignity
of a Royal chaplain, and if we are
to believe Dr. Lechler's arguments,
Wiclif had a seat in the "Good Parliament" of 1366 as a clerical expert, or, as
it is now termed, as a Government Com-
missioner. The Lords vehemently opposed Urban's claim, and finally rejected
it unanimously, adding, that if the Pope

should insist on his claims, they were prepared to resist by force with all their might.

In this quarrel Wiclif had drawn upon himself the attacks of an anonymous writer. In a pamphlet still extant, which was issued in the form of a Report of the parliamentary debate, he answers his opponent by introducing six Lords as speakers, and making them the mouthpieces of his own opinions on the great doctrine of the relation of Church and State. Amongst the doctrines which some months later were embodied by him in his book "On the Divine Dominion," is to be found the famous theory of government, which furnishes the key to all the labours he had to undergo at this period of his life, when he had become the defender of national liberty. They are characteristic enough to be adduced here in a short extract. Wiclif maintained that " God Himself is the chief Lord of all things or

possessions. From Him every man
holds, as far as any true rights of
ownership are concerned, and to Him
he must do service. If he fail in this
service—that is, if he fall into mortal
sin—he forfeits his rights. For there
are two titles by which a man holds
temporal goods: the title of *original*
justice, and that of *earthly* justice. By
the title of original justice Christ possessed all worldly goods, as Augustine
often says; by that title—the title of
grace—all things belong to the just,
but civil possession has little to do
with that title. For all men sin, and by
breaking the obedience to God such a
title is forfeited." In actual practice,
of course, this forfeiture could not
always be enforced, God Himself per-
mitting to the wicked power. God
thus, as it were, submits to the evil,
or, in Wiclif's own scholastic phrase,
so strangely misunderstood afterwards,
"God must obey the devil." All
rulers and owners, therefore, hold

direct from God, as their "dominus capitalis," or, to use Wiclif's own expression "Dominion is founded in Grace." " In Him alone dominion in its highest sense rests; He is the suzerain of the universe, who has delegated His own power to no vicegerent, but deals out His rule, in fief as it were, to man on condition of obedience to His commandments. If, therefore, God Himself has allotted portions of dominion to man, it is not granted to one man, His vicar on earth, as the Pope alleged, but to all. The King is as truly God's vicar as the Pope, and his power as sacred as the ecclesiastical, and as complete over temporal things—even the temporalities of the Church—as that of the Pope over temporal things." The sovereignty, therefore, derived by the Pope over all earthly authorities has never been delegated by God to any man, and if any one were to be held to be Christ's vicar on earth—and Wiclif was prepared to

allow this title to the Pope—the title
is equally applicable to the temporal
as to the spiritual chief. " The King
is as much bound by his office to see
that temporal goods are not wasted or
misapplied by the clergy, as the latter
is to direct the spiritual affairs of the
King; and, while the King and the
Pope are indeed supreme each in his
own department, every Christian man
holds directly of God—the final and
irreversible appeal is therefore to the
court, not of Rome, but of Heaven." [1]

If this doctrine of Dominion—the
denying to the Pope the right of con-
trol over all earthly things—could be
proved, the old quarrel between the
temporal and spiritual power of Western Christianity would be set at rest,
for neither Pope nor King could any

[1] For more particulars on this point and
the following, see Matthew, English Works,
pp. xxxii. ff. ; Burrows, Wiclif's Place,
pp. 14 ff.; Vaughan, John de Wycliffe, Monogr.
pp. 460, 529 ff. ; and Lechler, Johann von
Wiclif, pp. 500 ff., to whom I owe much.

longer be looked upon as a fountain of temporal authority. But there were other and even greater consequences rising out of this new doctrine; on the one hand, the emancipation of the individual conscience from the authority of King or Pope, and on the other, the independence of the Church of Christ from the State, and, as a consequence, her restoration to her former purity.

Principles of this ideal kind, brought forward by Wiclif with a surpassing amount of learning and acumen, which even his opponents acknowledged, deeply moved the minds of his own and succeeding generations. That his enemies should resent them as revolutionary was only natural. We must, therefore, not wonder that the fear, the hatred, and the persecutions of a degenerate hierarchy rallied against the Reformer who in such an outspoken manner opposed its exorbitant demands —temporal as well as spiritual—on the nation.

On the other hand, a more powerful

champion of the national and Royal privileges could scarcely be conceived in the struggle on which Edward and his Parliament had entered against the long continued extortions of the Pope. By his manful resistance to foreign encroachments of any kind Wiclif had become the advocate of the national aspirations and one of the foremost political leaders of the day. Where the opportunity of asserting the national right presented itself, he would unhesitatingly step into the front rank of warriors. Thus in 1372, when the Pope had sent one Arnold Garnier into England as his nuncio and receiver of the Papal dues, Wiclif in a public paper violently attacked this agent. Garnier had been subjected to an oath " to be true and loyal to the King ; to keep the council informed of all letters, Papal or other, that he received, and neither to send money out of the realm, nor himself to leave it without special license ; that he would neither

himself, nor permit other, to do anything which could possibly be dis-
pleasing or prejudicial to the King's
royal majesty, his royal laws and
rights, or to any one of his subjects."
Though having taken this oath in the
most formal and emphatic manner,
Garnier did not care to keep it in its
literal sense, and thus enabled Wiclif
to show that again by this man's agency
the interests of the King and the nation
had been grossly interfered with ; that
the oath "had been broken in almost
every particular ; the poor have been
robbed of their money; the Church
stripped of the alms given for its support ; the prosperity of the kingdom
seriously diminished ; God Himself
dishonoured ; Church services crip-
pled ; and the very nature of an oath
depraved." He then goes on to ex-
pose the usual prevarication on this
point, the Papal extortions and claims
to foreign money, and winds up by
styling the Pope "errabilis."

Two years after this literary struggle, in 1374, Wiclif was commissioned by Royal command to a legation sent out by Edward III. to Bruges, in Flanders, to meet the agents of Gregory XI. and to treat with them on the practice of Papal Provisions and a number of other abuses of a similar kind. In this embassy he took the second place, the Bishop of Bangor being its leader. The main object, however, for which the commission was sent was not attained; the old system continued, and in later years gave rise to repeated remonstrances on the part of the English Parliament.

Nevertheless this embassy to Bruges became in more than one respect of momentous import to Wiclif. Everything in this visit was fitted to ripen in such a mind the process that made Wiclif gradually the fiercest antagonist of Rome. Here opportunity was given him for watching the intellectual forces which then moved Christianity.

Coming into personal contact with the Papal envoys, all leading ecclesiastics of France, Spain, and Italy, he gained a closer insight than he had previously possessed into the motives and the corrupt practices of the Court of Avignon. On the other hand, it was this stay at Bruges, where at this very time a Royal Commission, with the Duke of Lancaster at its head, was negotiating for peace with the French ambassadors, that brought him into near relation to John of Gaunt, who, more on political than on religious grounds, became afterwards his protector.

From the old King, who by this time had become nearly imbecile, and from the good Prince of Wales, whose health was entirely broken, Wiclif had nothing to expect; soon he was to find that he needed influential friends to join him. On his return to England from Bruges, with deepened aversion to the prevailing ecclesiastical system, he began to speak in the tone of a Reformer. He is plain, homely, vigorous, sometimes rough, but always to the point. In one of his tracts of this period, he styles the Pope the "Antichrist, the proud, worldly priest of Rome, and the most cursed of clippers and cut-purses."

It could not, therefore, be wondered at that the hierarchy began to be stirred by the challenge of his audacious language and doctrine. The prelates resolved to move against him, and the more so as some new conclusions which he published went in the old track " that the Pope has no more power in binding and loosing than any other simple priest ; that endowments cannot be given in perpetuity, it being always right to withdraw them from unworthy holders ; and that temporal lords may take away the possessions of the clergy if pressed by necessity."

This doctrine was boldly preached by the Reformer himself in Oxford and London, and by his disciples in

other places of the country. The
sympathy and support of many knights
who "savoren myche þe gospel," and
of men of high rank, such as the Duke
of Lancaster and the Earl Marshal,
Lord Henry Percy, was on his side
when his bold challenge was taken up
by the clerical party. With the energetic Bishop of London (Courtenay)
at their head, the ecclesiastical digni-
taries stirred up the Archbishop of
Canterbury, who sent Wiclif a summons
to appear before Courtenay on February
23rd, 1377, in S. Paul's Cathedral.
Wiclif consented to make his appear-
ance there, and, accompanied by the
Duke, Lord Percy, and a great retinue,
they came up through Fleet Street and
Ludgate Hill to crowded S. Paul's
Churchyard. When the party reached
the door of the cathedral a grand
scene ensued.

The approach of the Reformer to
the presence of his judges had become
difficult, the cathedral being filled with

the populace, and when the ducal party made their way in a noisy and violent manner through the assembly, the fury of the proud Courtenay broke out into storm.

"Lord Percy," he said, "if I had known what maisteries you would have kept in the Church I would have stopped you out from coming hither."

Duke of Lancaster—" He shall keep such maisteries here though you say nay."

Lord Percy—"Wiclif, sit down, for you have many things to answer to, and you need to repose yourself on a soft seat."

Courtenay—" It is unreasonable that one cited before his ordinary should sit down during his answer. He must and shall stand."

Duke of L.—"The Lord Percy's motion for Wiclif is but reasonable. And as for you, my Lord Bishop, who are grown so proud and arrogant, I will bring down the pride, not of you alone, but of all the prelacy in England."

Courtenay—" Do your worst, sir."

Duke of L.—"Thou bearest thyself so brag upon thy parents,[1] which shall not be able to help thee. They shall have enough to do to help themselves."

Courtenay—"My confidence is not in my parents nor in any man else, but only in God, in Whom I trust, by Whose assistance I will be bold to speak the truth."

Duke of L.—"Rather than I will take those words at his hands I will pluck the Bishop by the hair out of the Church."

These violent words of the Duke were spoken in an undertone, nevertheless they had been heard by some bystanders and had caused an extraordinary excitement among the citizens present. In the tumult which followed, the Court broke up in confusion and without having decided anything in the cause of the Reformer, who was safely

[1] The powerful Hugh Courtenay, Earl of Devonshire, was the Bishop's father.

accompanied home by the noblemen through the crowded streets.

The first blow that came from the hierarchy had thus failed; the heretic had not been silenced, and his position remained as strong as before the attack. A second step made by the prelates in the same direction was accompanied by a similar result. Soon after the scene in S. Paul's, fifty conclusions taken from Wiclif's works had been sent to the Pope, then in Rome, and of these nineteen were selected to form a new charge of heresy against the Reformer. By means of no less than five bulls issued at once and directed to the King, the Primate, the Bishop of London, and the University, the Pope made an attempt to bring the matter finally to an issue. But the bulls met with an ambiguous reception in England. The king had died in the meantime, so his bull had missed its purpose; the University treated its own with contempt; the citizens of London had returned to their former regard for Wiclif; and by a new judgment as to the right of the Parliament to withhold money from the Pope when required for the defence of the realm, Wiclif had also recovered the confidence and sympathy of Parliament.

A synod assembled in Archbishop Sudbury's Chapel at Lambeth was broken into by the Londoners, and a message arrived from the Princess Regent prohibiting procedure against the defendant; this shook the Prelates as a reed in the wind, and they became soft as oil in their speech. With such fear they were " struck that they became as a man that heareth not, and in whose mouth are no reproofs."

Soon afterwards the news of the Pope's death arrived in England. This caused the Bishops to stop the persecution, and no further action was taken upon the five Papal bulls.

II.

REFORMER.

HE critical condition of Western Christendom at this time exercised a momentous influence upon Wiclif. It made him in some ways a new man and determined in a great measure the character of his subsequent action. Hitherto he had come forward as a national leader repelling Papal encroachments on English privileges. He had attacked the corrupt politics of the Church, while the person of the Pope continued to be venerated by him. But in 1378 the spectacle of

two rival Popes excommunicating and
preaching crusades against one another,
pushed him forward in the line of opposition, and made him now pass from
political to theological ground.

The Great Schism taught him that
he must appeal to the world in a wholly
different manner. His labour as a
political writer he saw had been success-
ful, but he must not stop short here;
for he was aware that professors and
politicians before him had done so and
failed to strike at the root of the evil.
His experience in the schools of Oxford
and in his political struggles had shown
him that the Church system of his time
was corrupt to its very core: so the
doctrine of the Church becomes now
the object of his attacks.

Shortly after the elevation of Urban
VI. to the Papal dignity at Rome, the
French Cardinals at Avignon had made
Clement VII. anti-pope. The two rivals
were at once at war; they excommuni-
cated each other; a crusade was pro-

claimed ; and the Mendicants who had
deeply plunged into this deadly contest
of the two spiritual leaders of Western
Christendom, promised numerous indulgences to those who were on the
point of taking up the causes of their
respective patrons : the Gregorian idea
of the unity of the Church was irre-
vocably gone.

Now when England, and indeed all
Christendom, was again overrun by
pardon-mongers, and difficulties arose
as to who was the right Pope, Wiclif,
who had hitherto acknowledged the
necessity and primacy of the Papal see,
began to proclaim that the Church
would be better off without a Pope.
By this conclusion he enters into the
theological field, and begins his new
battle against the numerous abuses of
the Church, which had hitherto formed
the main hindrance to a purer and
more evangelic life among the common
people. His first blows were directed
against the Papacy itself and its agents ;

he then proceeded to attack the whole Church system of the time. Once freed from the trammels of unquestioning belief, " his mind worked fast in its career of reformation." The magnificence and worldliness of Prelates and Friars, who lived in " Cain's Castles " a luxurious life ; the prevalence of unworthy influences and simony in the presentation to benefices; the extortions and abuses of the bishops' and archdeacons' courts, especially the practice of enacting fines for incontinence and other sins, instead of requiring amendment ; pilgrimages to the shrines of the Saints; worship of their images; worship of the Saints themselves — all these things were successively denounced by him.[1]   At the same time, the privilege of the Church to grant indulgences, and to fill, by the money thus obtained, the purses of the numerous pardon-sellers ;

[1] In the second part of this little volume the reader will find some of Wiclif's arguments against these teachings, contained in short extracts from his works.

the fiction of a spiritual treasure in heaven collected by the Saints and put at the disposal of the Pope ; and, in connection with this false doctrine, the Letters of fraternity, special prayers, and still masses, offered him a wide scope for his denunciation. " To enforce private confession," he declared, " is a practice novel as well as mischievous ; it is by the penitence and confession to God Himself, that pardon of our sins is granted. All merit is in the hands of God, who keeps to Himself the distribution of it. Not only so, but the Pope cannot know the real state of a man, and may grant pardon to one who is in mortal sin and unable to profit by the gift."

All this was new language, plain fearless, trenchant, that went home to the heart of the people. There had been some men before Wiclif who had been fully awake to these abuses, and to the evil that threatened the religious life of the people ; stricter discipline, they had thought, and the withdrawal of privileges, indulgences, provisions, and the like, should be applied to heal the wound. There had also been men who were staunch believers in the Pope and his authority, and who, at the same time, had bitterly complained of, or boldly inveighed against, the evil discipline then in existence. Side by side with them in this spiritual battle fought Wiclif, armed, however, to advantage with the keenness of his language and with the sharpness of his deeper insight. But what made his attacks appear in a new light was his attempt to strike the system at its root, by falling back on the institutions and teaching of the Divine Gospel, and by attacking not the individual, but the government and the constitution of the Church. It was the *principle* he was at war with. No one before him had striven with such unreserved determination to bring back the Church from the outward lifeless forms, to urge her regeneration in accordance with Holy Scripture, and thus to renew the foundation on which it stood. In him the essential ideas and the evangelical aims of all those who before him had found themselves in opposition to the Church had their representative; in the " doctor evangelicus " the currents of the reforming spirit of the Middle Ages meet, and by his fundamental opposition to the doctrine of the Church he becomes the greatest of the Pre-reformers.

He entered upon the dangerous ground of doctrine when he struck at the evil principles that were underlying the corrupt practices of the Church. By his former attacks he could appeal to the moral sense of laymen, and the spiritual instincts of his audience were on his side. Into the subtleties of a doctrinal question, however, the popular mind, that did not care for scholastic distinctions, such as of substance and accidents, was not able to follow him, and the sympathies which the English people had entertained for the maintainer of their national liberties began to cease.

On the other hand, his attack on Transubstantiation aroused his old adversaries, the Bishops and the Mendicants, against him. In a great many tracts in English and Latin he had exposed the evil doings of the latter, and had now to find that the Friars made the best of the opportunity offered to them of playing the part of the defenders of Church doctrine, rather than of their own evil practices.

In the spring of 1381, while his great work of translating the Bible into English, and of organizing the institute of his " Poor Priests " was probably going on, he published in Oxford a paper of twelve propositions, denying that great doctrine upon which the supremacy of the priestly Church of the Middle Ages rested—the Romish theory of Transubstantiation.

It is by this discussion on the prin-
cipal doctrine of the whole Romish
system that Wiclif became the leader
of that great spiritual movement which
ended more than a hundred years afterwards by establishing for every Pro-
testant Christian freedom of conscience,
and by which "the great mass of the
Teutonic peoples was severed from the
general body of the Catholic Church."

This new act was the bolder in that
Wiclif undertook it quite alone, and
supported by none of his former
friends. In the University also the
influence of the Regulars had become
victorious, and its Chancellor was compelled to take measures against the
heretical preacher. His conclusions
were condemned.

Wiclif was just engaged in some
disputations on the truth of his teaching in the schools of the Augustines,
when the academical condemnation
was published in his presence. If we
are to believe Walden, his opponent,

he was startled a moment when he heard the condemnation, but soon rallied, and declared that neither the Chancellor nor any one of his party could refute his opinions. A few days later the Duke of Lancaster came down to Oxford and confirmed the Chancellor's sentence by forbidding Wiclif to speak any more on the subject. This prohibition of the Duke he met with an open avowal of his views on the matter, and published his " Confession," which he closes with the proud and famous words, " I trust that in the end Truth will conquer." In this "Confession" the main points of his view on the matter are given. Turning against the blasphemy of the received doctrine that the body of Christ is made by the priest, the Creator by His creature, he nevertheless maintains that while the substance of the bread remains bread after being consecrated by the priest, it becomes in some sense, as bread, the body of

Christ. The words, "This is my body," have their meaning, the bread remaining to the last true bread in the *natural* sense, while in the *figurative* sense it is the body of the Lord, as when Christ said to St. John, "This is Elias." Thus the body and the blood of Christ *are really and indeed present*, the elements being no mere signs, but "signa efficacia," *i.e.*, we receive the body not *corporeally*, substantially, but *spiritually*, not by reason, but by faith. "It is the Spirit that quickeneth." Christ, although everywhere present, is in the Blessed Sacrament "distinctively, that is sacramentally, present," not locally, as His body is in heaven, yet as the bread itself is there in the sacrament, the body of Christ is likewise present for the believer. By this teaching the difficulty of explaining he mode of the presence is not met, some may say; but "it is not greater," has been truly replied, "in this system than it is in the Bible itself, or in the teaching of our great divines, as, for instance, Hooker and Waterland, or in the Articles of our own Church. Indeed, the doctrine to be found in the Church formularies is wonderfully similar to that of Wiclif, if not identical with it."

A flood of denunciation in the form of theological pamphlets now descended upon him from the Regulars. But, when the tide was highest, the Secular party in the University came forward and turned it in his favour. Their common enmity against the Regular monks told in the University elections of the annual officers, and the most influential members—Chancellor and Proctor—were selected from those professors who favoured Wiclif's teachings. Thus by tacitly adopting his cause the University once again withdrew its persecution, and troubled him no more.

But Wiclif by this time did not expect further support from the wealthy and learned men from whom he had

hitherto received assistance. He ven-
tured on quite a new step that in the
whole history of England had never
been attempted by any political or intellectual leader before him : he appealed to the nation at large. In
the tongue of the people tract after
tract on the Eucharist, the Friars, the
Prelates, the Pope, the crusade to
Flanders, were issued with amazing
rapidity. He had addressed his academical hearers in Latin. This he now
set aside, and " by a transition which
marks the wonderful genius of the
man, the schoolman was transformed
into the pamphleteer." He stepped in
at Chaucer's side as the father of later
English prose, and brought about by
these tracts, in which the speech of
the peasant and the trader of the
day is embodied, a new epoch in the
history of the English language. The
pathos of his rough, clear, homely
speech, coloured with the picturesque
phraseology of the Bible, the terse,

vehement sentences, the stinging sar-
casm, the fine antitheses, went home to
the heart of the people who could read
or hear, and "roused the dullest mind
like a whip."

But the more his influence on the
people made itself felt and the more
the Londoners and the University
became infected with "Lollardism,"
the more angry grew the Regulars,
now led by Wiclif's old adversary
Courtenay, who after Sudbury's sudden
death at the hands of Wat Tyler's
rebels had become Archbishop of Canterbury. "Pontius Pilate and Herod
are made friends to-day"—so he commented bitterly on the new union
which for the purpose of resisting their
common foe had sprung up between
the Prelates and the Mendicant Orders,
who had so long been at variance with
each other. "Since they have made a
heretic of Christ, it is an easy inference
for them to count simple Christians
heretics."

In May, 1382, a provincial council
was convened by the new primate at
Blackfriars, in London, a council made
memorable by the incident of an earthquake, which shook the whole city and
frightened every prelate but the resolute and ready Courtenay. He gave
a different meaning to the incident,
saying that the dispersion of ill-humours produced by such convulsions
of the earth was a good omen, signify-
ing the expulsion of ill-humours from
the Church. Thus the courage of the
wavering members was quickly restored,
and without summoning the Reformer
into its presence, the " Council of the
Earthquake " condemned after " the
good deliberation of three days," twenty-
four conclusions which had been taken
for the purpose out of Wiclif's writings.
Ten of the doctrines were condemned
as heretical, the remaining as erroneous.
The former, according to Wilkins,
related to the Sacrament of the Altar,
as being perfected without any change

in the substance of bread and wine ;
to priests and bishops, as ceasing to be
such on falling into deadly sin ; to
auricular confession, as unnecessary;
to ecclesiastical endowments as unlawful ; and to the claims of the Pope,
when he shall happen to be a depraved
man, as being derived solely from the
edict of Cæsar, and not at all from the
authority of the Gospel. The erroneous propositions are those which declare that "a prelate excommunicating
any one, without knowing him to be
condemned of God, is himself a heretic
and excommunicated ; that to prohibit
appeals from the tribunal of the clergy
to that of the King is to withhold from
the Sovereign the allegiance due to him ;
that priests and deacons all possess
authority to preach the gospel, without
waiting for the license of popes or
prelates ; that to abstain from preaching the gospel for fear of clerical
censure must be to appear in the day
of doom under the guilt of treason

against Christ; that temporal lords may deprive a delinquent clergy from their possessions; that tithes are simply alms to be offered as the judgment or conscience of the laity may determine, and only as the clergyman shall be devout and deserving; and finally, that the institution of the religious orders is contrary to Holy Scripture, and being sinful in itself tends in many ways to what is sinful."

The condemnation having been published in London and Oxford, the fierce Archbishop turned his anger upon the University as the fount and centre of the new doctrine. There a struggle commenced, the issues of which have proved for more than one reason memorable in the whole history of the great school. The author of the heretical propositions was compelled to withdraw from Oxford, where a search for copies of his works was ordered. He retired to the rectory of Lutterworth and devoted his time, so far as his bodily health

allowed him, to his parish work, being
troubled no more by the action of so
bold an antagonist as Courtenay.
"Nothing marks more strongly," has
been truly said, "the grandeur of
Wiclif's position as the last of the
great schoolmen than the reluctance
of this proud and energetic primate to
take, even after his triumph over Oxford,
extreme measures against the head of
Lollardy." Against his party in the
University, however, the strictest measures were taken, this time without
being objected to by John of Gaunt
and the Royal Court.

Here in Oxford Hereford had maintained the truth of his Master's teaching in an English sermon at S. Frides-
wide's, and Repyngdon had declared
the Lollards to be "holy priests."
"The clerical order," he had cried,
"was better when it was but nine
years old than now that it has grown
to a thousand years and more." "There
is no idolatry," a third, James William,

had exclaimed, in the presence of the Chancellor, Robert Rigge, "save in the Sacrament of the Altar." " You speak like a wise man," Rigge had replied.

This perversity of opinion had made the Regulars take the matter in hand. The proceedings of Hereford, Repyngdon, Aston, and Bedeman, Wiclif's first " Poor Priests," by whose agency Wiclifism had now become a power through town and country, were complained of by the Regulars in a paper which they presented to the king. The proud Courtenay himself now turned his action against the suspected Chancellor Rigge. Not willing to bear defiance tamely, he summoned him to Lambeth, wrested from him, after a short resistance, complete submission, and enacted from him a pledge to suppress Lollardism in the University. When the letters condemning the tenets of Wiclif were handed to Rigge, he objected : " I dare not publish them in the University, on fear of death ;" to

3 *

which the Primate replied : " Then is your University in open favour with heresy, if it does not suffer the Catholic truth to be proclaimed within its walls."

Rigge knew his University. The publication of the episcopal injunction set Oxford in a blaze, the bulk of the students siding with the Lollards, and exclaiming against the friars that " they wished to destroy the University." But the Crown supported Courtenay's decrees by issuing a royal writ, which ordered "the instant banishment of all favourers of Wiclif, with the seizure of all Lollard books, on pain of forfeiture of the University privileges."

Thus the suppression of Wiclif and his party in the University was completed through the agency of the monks and prelates, and his cause " received a blow from which it seems never to have thoroughly recovered." But, it should be added, the religious freedom, the intellectual independence, and the privileges of self-government had like-

wise been lost. The constitution of
the great school had been broken into
by the clerical party, and the University
authorities had lost the battle. In the
University itself, along with the death
of religious freedom, "all traces of intellectual life suddenly disappear. The
century which followed the triumphs of
Courtenay is the most barren in its
annals, nor was the sleep of the University broken till the advent of the New
Learning restored to it some of the life
and liberty which the Primate had so
roughly trodden out."

HILE thus Wiclif—having
retired to the quiet cure
of Lutterworth — was
doing the work of a sim-
ple priest, the seeds of
his teaching and writing began to be dispersed throughout the country through
the agency of his "Travelling Poor
Priests."

Before our mind's eye the picture of these sturdy, freespoken, and popular preachers of the fourteenth century arises: barefooted, clothed in long habits of red colour, in their hands the pilgrim's staff, the sackcloth being the emblem of hard work and poverty, they travel from town to town, from market to market, from village to village ; and in churches, chapels, mass-houses, wherever an audience may be gathered, to merchant, trader, mechanic, and peasant, they preach "Goddis lawe." No name could be more suited to them than that of " Poor Priests." To prelates and abbots, rectors and curates, monks and friars, they became objects of hatred, while with the people their favour and influence were ever on the increase. It is to the father of English poetry that we owe the picture of the new type of parson :

" A good man ther was of religioun,
　That was a poure persone [1] of a toun :

[1] Parson.

But riche he was of holy thought and werk —
He was also a lerned man, a clerk,
That Cristes gospel trewely wolde preche.
Benigne he was, and wonder diligent,
And in adversite ful patient.
Ful loth were him to cursen for his tithe
But rather wolde he yeven out of doute
Unto his poure parishens aboute,
Of his offring, and eke of his substance.
He coude a litel thing have suffisance.
Wide was his parish, and houses fer asonder,
But he ne left nought for no rain ne thonder,
In sikenesse and in mischief to visite
The ferrest in his parish, moche and lite,[1]
Upon his fete, and in his hand a staf.
This noble ensample to his shepe he yaf,
That first he wrought, and afterwards he
taught.
Out of the gospel he the wordes caught.
For if a preest be foule, on whom we trust,
No wonder is a lewed man to rust :
And shame it is, if that a preest take kepe,
To see a shitten shepherd, and clene sheep.
He was a shepherd, and no mercenarie
He was to a sinful men not dispitous
Ne of his speche dangerous ne digne,[2]
But in his teching discrete and benigne.
To drawen folk to heven, with fairenesse,
By good ensample, was his besinesse ;
But it were any persone obstinat,

---

[1] High and low.   [2] Proud.

What so he were of highe, or low estat
Him wolde he snibben sharply for the nones [1]
A better preest I trowe that nowher non is.
For Cristes lore, and his apostles twelve,
He taught, but first he folwed it himselve."

What was the origin of this new order of religious agents, who, in the whole of English history, were without precedent? As often happens in history, great spiritual movements come under our notice, not indeed as a full-developed product, but when their organization is in full activity; often their origin remains hidden in the mist of past years.

It is in Archbishop Courtenay's mandate to the Bishop of London (1382) that these men appear for the first time. He denounces them as 'unauthorised itinerant preachers, who teach erroneous, yea, heretical assertions publicly, not only in churches, but also in public squares, and other profane places; and who do this under

---

[1] Occasion.

the guise of great holiness, but without
having obtained any episcopal or papal
authorisation." From these expressions,
which show the system in full operation, we may gather that the formation
of the order must lie some years back.
There is evidence, though not quite
unimpeachable, that as early as 1375,
Wiclif superintended the training of
some such preachers; in 1378, when
some parts of the English Bible had
been finished, the order seems to have
reached its full development; in 1380,
at least, it may be inferred from
Knighton's chronicle, that the priests
were travelling over a great part of
England.

Wiclif's aim in sending forth these
"good priests," who were formed on
his ideal of the Christian ministry, and
taught in God's law, was to supply the
defects of the regular parson of the
time, who, instead of preaching the
Word of God, and devoting himself to
the spiritual care of his flock, contented

himself with the formal reading of Church services. A former attempt to meet the prevailing want by founding the Mendicant's Order had proved a failure ; for the Dominicans, by their very constitution "preachers," as well as the Franciscans, to whom the education of the rich and the mission work among the poor had been entrusted, had degenerated into an avaricious set of men, whose unworthy efforts to gain the popular favour had won for them the unenviable reputation of furnishing the most assailable butt for popular satire. So the task had still to be done ; and Wiclif's " Poor Priests," though no reproduction of the Mendicants, succeeded in fulfilling what the friars had so completely failed to perform.

They formed no monkish order ; they were not bound by irrevocable vows, but while abstaining from all worldly occupation, as trading, hunting, ploughing, &c., they devoted them-

selves entirely to the preaching of the
Gospel in English, and to prayer. In
the first stage of the institution they
were taken from the order of secular
priests, graduates and undergraduates
of Oxford. Later on, laymen also were
sent out, and if we read aright some
passages in Wiclif's unpublished works
in the Vienna collection, the Reformer
himself had sanctioned the mission of
the lay-priest before his death. From
its beginning Oxford had been the
centre of their mission ; afterwards,
when Wiclif had retired to Leicestershire, the town of Leicester appears, in
contemporary chronicles, as another
cradle of the mission. Numerous tracts
have been left to us by the Reformer
which refer to the " priests," either by
giving them advice on the mode of
their preaching, or by defending their
labours against their adversaries. Thus
Wiclif had become the founder of a
new order whose members combined
the priest with the layman, and resem-

bled in all practical points "Wesley's lay-preachers as they were when his strong hand was upon them."

While thus by the institution of his "Poor Priests" the Reformer had succeeded in bringing the popular mind into closer contact with the pure Gospel, he had secured to himself another means of meeting the spiritual wants of the layman by his translation of the Bible into English.

There can be no doubt that, while we are not able to determine the exact share Wiclif had in this vast work, the first conception, as well as the practical scheme of translating the Bible, is due to him. We now know that he himself took part in the translation, and that the accomplishment of the whole work must be attributed to his zeal and encouragement, to his intense energy, and to the extraordinary power of his resolute will.

Down to the middle of the fourteenth century (1360), in natural conse-

quence of the priestly efforts to withhold the Scriptures from the layman,
no part of the Bible, with the single
exception of the Psalms, had been
translated into English. On the other
hand we know for certain that from
thirty to forty years later a prose ver-
sion of the *whole* Bible, including the
apocryphal books, had not only been
completed, but was in circulation
among, and eagerly read by, English
laymen.

It is to Wiclif that England owes
this invaluable gift, the outcome of a
noble and novel conception ; *novel* in
two respects, for it had for its object
the literal translation of the whole
Bible, without gloss or commentary,
and it was meant to be *in every man's
hand*. For many reasons which need
not be adduced here, an undertaking
of this kind could not be expected from
the Papal Church, which had reserved
for itself sole and infallible authority in
determining the meaning of the Word

of God. To this duty of the clergy to withhold the Bible from their flock, Knighton, the chronicler of this period, bears testimony, which at the same time is decisive as to the part Wiclif had taken in placing the English Bible in the hands of the people. " Christ," he says, "delivered His Gospel to the clergy and doctors of the Church, but this Master John Wiclif translated it out of Latin into English, and thus laid it out more open to the laity, and to women who could read, than it had formerly been to the most learned of the clergy, even to those of them that had the best understanding. In this way the gospel-pearl is cast abroad, and trodden under foot of swine, and that which was before precious both to clergy and laity, is rendered, as it were, to the common jest of both. The jewel of the Church is turned into the sport of the people, and what had hitherto been the choice gift of the clergy and of divines, is made for ever

common to the laity." In the face of
this evidence there can be no doubt
that the translation is Wiclif's work.
To the same effect is a letter addressed
by Archbishop Arundel to the Pope
John XXIII. in 1412, in which Wiclif
is said to have " impugned with all his
power the creed and the teaching of
the Church, and, in order to fulfil the
measure of his wickedness, to have
invented the translation of the Bible
into the mother tongue." John Hus
also, in his reply to John Stokes, is
witness that "Wyclif translated the
whole gospel from the Latin into the
English language."

As to the date, however, when the
work was taken up, no certainty can as
yet be arrived at. The evidence we
have is of merely a negative kind ; in all
the charges brought forward against
Wiclif's obnoxious teaching in 1377,
1381, and 1382, no mention of the
translation is made. Only in 1381, when
the Reformer was silenced in Oxford

in some of his own numerous tracts he poured forth from his solitude, positive allusions to the subject occur. In one of his sermons he speaks of "a great bishop of the English being deeply incensed because God's law is written *in English to lewd men* (laymen). He pursueth a certain priest, because he writeth to men this English, and summoneth him, and traveleth him. And thus he pursueth another priest by the help of Monks and Friars, because he preacheth Christ's gospel freely and without fables." Bishop Courtenay and the two priests, Hereford and Aston, in all probability are meant here. By this time, therefore, Wiclif had the impression that Courtenay was incensed to prosecute the priests by a suspicion of their intention to put "God's law written in English" into the hands of the laymen; in any case, Wiclif knew that as early as 1381 Hereford was engaged in the labour of translating.

Naturally the New Testament was first taken in hand. That this translation is Wiclif's own work is proved not only by the similarity between the style of the Gospels and that of other genuine Wiclifian parts, but likewise by the evidence furnished by Hus's reply to Stokes ("Whole Gospel," p. 94). Prologues agreeing with those commonly found in Latin transcripts of the 14th century were added perhaps by another hand. While the New Testament was in progress, or shortly after its completion, the Old Testament was taken in hand by Nicholas Hereford, one of Wiclif's disciples, whose original MS. is still preserved in the Bodleian library. A second MS., likewise in the Bodleian, which was copied from the former before its correction, contains Hereford's name ("explicit tranlacōn nicholay herford"), and the curious coincidence that both MSS. run on to Baruch iii. 20, where the text suddenly breaks off, shows that the translator was stopped in the midst of his work.. Now Hereford, who after Wiclif's condemnation in May, 1382, had come to the front in Oxford, was silenced in June by a Provincial Council, excommunicated, and after having appealed to the Pope he went, according to Knighton, to Italy to defend himself before the Pontiff. Thus the breaking off of the text may be conveniently explained. At the same time we may infer that the translation of the New Testament had been finished by Wiclif in June, 1382, when Hereford had advanced already to the apocryphal books of the Old Testament. Very probably the continuation of Hereford's work is by Wiclif's own hand.

The translation of the whole Bible having been thus completed, the next care was to make it known as far, and to render it as useful, as possible. For this end " A Table of the Portions of Scripture read as the Epistles and

Gospels of the Church Service on the Sundays, Feasts, and Fasts of the Year," was framed. This table was inserted in certain copies of the newly translated Bible, and the passages were marked in the text by letters placed in the margin, over against the beginning and end of the several portions; or sometimes the margin contained a rubric, stating at length the service for which the lesson was appointed. To some copies of the New Testament such portions of the Old were annexed as were used in the Church service instead of the Epistles. In order also to render those parts of Scripture in most frequent use accessible at less cost, books were written containing nothing more than the Gospels and Epistles read in the service of the Mass."

All this being done without the basis of clear principles of translation, within comparatively short time, by different hands and under unfavourable circumstances, it was only natural that the

work was not faultless. But Wiclif
was not the man to stop short when
the task was only half done. We now
know that Hereford's books differed
in style from the rest, his translation
being extremely literal, occasionally
obscure, and sometimes incorrect. We
cannot be surprised, therefore, that
Wiclif had under consideration a revision of the whole translation. Whether
he lived to see this revision completed
is not quite certain. While it owed its
execution to his suggestion and encouragement, it seems to have been
finished only four years after his death,
in 1388, by his friend John Purvey,
who was at the same time his curate
in Lutterworth. By this time numerous copies of both versions, in particular of the New Testament, were in
circulation. That this revised translation found many readers may be
gathered from the fact that we still
have upwards of a hundred and fifty
copies of it preserved in English

libraries. This wide circulation must also account for the fact that for a long time obscurity lay on Wiclif's own labour, the first translation, and that through the frequent publication of Purvey's work, for which the name "Wiclif's Bible" was in general use until about 1850, the genuine work of the Reformer had fallen into oblivion.

From Forshall and Madden's investigations we now know that the vast scheme of procuring an English Bible for the English reader is not only due to Wiclif in regard to its original conception, but also in the actual execution of the most important section, and in the supervision of what had been done by others. It was a deed which stands for more than it seems, and, we may add, which has performed more than it first promised. For the translators saw "no more all that was involved in what they did than our ancestors saw all that was included in the provisions of the Magna Charta." And indeed, in

more than one respect, the English
Bible has become for the English
people the great charter of its religious freedom. For the execution of
Wiclif's idea became a historical fact
pregnant with principles which a hundred and fifty years later proved the most
powerful agents in influencing the
thought of Europe. These principles
were the liberation of the individual
from the hands of the priest, the Right
of Private Judgment, the Sufficiency of
Holy Scripture with regard to salvation, and the transfer of the ultimate
authority in religious matters from the
Papal Church to the single believer.

In bringing forward these grand
principles on which the spiritual as
well as the intellectual life of our
present generation rests, Wiclif over-
stepped the bounds of his own country
and age, and as a prophet and a religious genius, anticipated that new spiritual life to which his own generation
was only gradually awakening. Com-

pared with the great men of his time,
he stands before us veiled in a sort of
lonely grandeur and mystery, which is
now slowly passing away, as we learn
more of him, of his doings and teachings, by the publication of his writings.

Nor should his translation of the
Bible be commented upon merely from
the religious standpoint. Like Luther's
Bible in German literature, it marks
an era in the English language;
Luther's translation opening the period
of the New-High-German, Wiclif's that
of Middle English; for it is no longer
Geoffrey Chaucer that we must regard
as the sole founder of our modern
English. Wiclif's life work secures
to him a claim of similar grandeur.
Chaucer's amusing and graceful stories,
illustrating the life and the manners of
his time, and told with a freshness and
joyousness of feeling that even Shake-
speare does not surpass, are inestimable
in their *historical and social* value.
Wiclif's Bible influenced in quite a

singular manner *the religious feeling*,
the inmost soul of the reader; Chaucer appealed *only to the cultured class*,
Wiclif *to all*, to the educated as well
as to the simple man. By thus introducing a new form of religious and
moral truths into all classes of society,
he opened the way for the new language
to far wider circles than Chaucer,
whose influence was more or less con-
fined to the few literary men of his
time.

F the last few years of his
life which he spent at
Lutterworth only little remains to be told. Here
he lived the quiet life of
a parish priest, no longer troubled by
his old enemies, who did not dare to
persecute him further.

From one of his polemical tracts recently published by the Wiclif Society,
an incident of this period of his life

which hitherto has been doubted is clearly established : he was summoned to appear before the Pope in Rome. But failing health hindered the " feeble and lame priest cited to Rome," because " the King of kings forces him and will not that he go." From this passage we see that the words were spoken by a man who was drawing near to the presence of a Judge higher and juster than he by whom he had been cited.

The terrible strain on his health, together with the exertions of continued studies and the feebleness of old age, at last had told on his powers : when hearing Mass in his church on Holy Innocent's day, 1384, he was struck for a second time with paralysis, and peacefully entered "into his fatherland " on December 31, 1384, " having lit a fire which should never be extinguished."

So John Wiclif died, the greatest Pre-reformer and one of the greatest men England has ever produced, a religious genius whose vestiges are to be found not only in the history of his own country, but in the spiritual history of mankind. Modern research proves that the Reformation neither of Germany, nor of England, nor of Bohemia, was a sudden outburst, but that its origin must be traced back into the past, and from no one can it with greater truth be said to have emanated than from John Wiclif the Englishman. In the spirit of this wonderful man Protestantism arose. By the greatness of his soul, the depth of his religious and national feeling, and the keenness of his intellect, he had become the leader of his people. When in England, towards the end of the Middle Ages, the new power of a national and religious awakening was struggling into existence, it was in Wiclif that it found its truest personification. Of him therefore in a singular manner is true what has been said of Luther, that " he held the mind and the spirit of his countrymen in his hand, and seemed to be the hero in whom his nation had become incarnate."

To renew and to bring home to our present generation the memory of so great a mind appears to me at this Quincentenary of his death a true national duty. Five hundred years ago the great English Doctor breathed his last; and surely after having benefitted for more than five hundred years from the spiritual blessings that went forth from this great genius, the people of England, otherwise so proud of its grand political and religious history, should at last awake to a sense of thankfulness towards the memory of one of her noblest sons. In truth England may be proud of him, who at the same time was the founder of her later prose, a national politician, an unsparing assailant of abuses, a bold and indefatigable controversialist, the founder of a new religious order, the great Reformer who did not shrink from

4*

questioning the truth of the Roman dogma, who broke through the traditions of the past, and who, while bound in his whole teaching by the Word of God, became the great advocate of the freedom of religious thought.

BOOK II.

ON GOD'S LAW.[1]

HRISTIAN men should stand to the death for the maintenance of Christ's Gospel, and the true understanding thereof, obtained by holy life and great study, and not set their faith nor trust in sinful

[1] The following extracts have been taken from Wiclif's unpublished Tract, *De Veritate Scripturæ Sacræ* (Cod. 1294 of the Vienna Library) from the *Trialogus* (Oxford Edition), the *Wykett*, and from Vaughan, *Tracts and Treatises of John Wykliffe*.

prelates and their clerks, nor in their understanding thereof.

*

*   *

*

Then they say that no man can know what is the Gospel but by the approving and confirming of the Church. But true men say that to their understanding this is full of falsehood. For Christian men have *certainty of belief by the gracious gift of Jesus Christ*, that *the truth* taught by Christ and His apostles is the Gospel, though all the clerks of Antichrist require men to believe the contrary, on pain of cursing, poisoning, and burning. And this belief is not founded on the Pope and his Cardinals, for then it might fail and be undone, but on Jesus Christ, God and Man, and on the Holy Trinity, and so it may never fail, except from his default who should love God and serve Him. The Christian's faith faileth not, and plainly because *they* are not the ground thereof, but *Jesus Christ is the ground thereof,* who is our God and our best Master, and *ready to teach true men all things profitable and needful to their souls.*

*
*   *
*

No Christian man is to admit that Holy Scripture be in any way false ; nor is he who understands Holy Scripture wrongly or badly, to allow that it is false. For its falsity does not lie in the Holy Scripture but in him who falsely interprets it. For if ever Holy Scripture had an impossible meaning, God Himself would have given it, and consequently it could not be called Holy.

*
*   *
*

If a son is not allowed to break the testament of his earthly father by contravening it or putting a wrong meaning into it, much less a Christian man

is allowed to vary from, or to dissolve
the incorrigible testament of God the
Father.

*
*   *
*

We believe the authors of the Old
Testament to have spoken out of an
inner inspiration coming from God's
mouth, not simply out of an inspiration
of faith or the sanctity of their life, nor
as authorized by the Church.

*
*   *
*

I wonder that some moderns put
calumny on those who say that they
have the Holy Spirit, while they them
selves assert to know that nobody
honours more the Holy Scripture than
they do. I for my part constantly
assert that, if a Christian man honours
the Holy Scripture merely like another
worldly man, he makes himself a god,
and consequently puts himself above
other Christian men.

The law of Christ must be loved in proportion as He who has given it, and, consequently, it is infinitely more to be honoured than human traditions. It is given to men by the uncreate Wisdom as the best suited means to bring peace among the people.

*

* *

*

Looking on the present state of the Church, we find that it would be better and of greater use to the Church if it were governed purely by the law of the Scripture than by human traditions mixed up with evangelical truths.

*

* *

*

God's law is the foundation for every catholic opinion, the example and mirror for to examine and to extinguish every error or heretical pravity. Therefore, even a slight error in this matter might bring about the death of the Church.

ON THE AUTHORITY
OF HOLY SCRIPTURE.

 HAVE learnt by expe-
rience the truth of what
you say (with reference
to my appeal to the
Scriptures). The chief
cause, beyond doubt, of the existing
state of things is our want of faith in
Holy Scripture. We do not sincerely
believe in the Lord Jesus Christ, or we
should abide by the authority of His
Word, in particular that of the Evan-

gelists, as of infinitely greater weight
than any other. Inasmuch as it is
the will of the Holy Spirit that our at-
tention should not be dispersed over a
large number of objects, but concen-
trated on one sufficient source of instruction, it is His pleasure that the
books of the Old and New Law should
be *read* and *studied*, and that men
should not be taken up with other
books, which, true as they may be, and
containing even Scripture truth, as they
may by implication, are not to be con-
fided in without caution and limitation.
Hence St. Austin often enjoins on his
readers not to place any faith in his
word or writings, except in so far as
they have their foundation in the Scriptures, wherein, as he often sayeth, all
truth either directly or implicitly is
contained. Of course we should judge
in this manner with reference to the
writings of other holy doctors, and
much more with reference to the
writings of the Roman Church, and of

her doctors in these later times. If we follow this rule, the Scriptures will be held in due respect. .

*

*   *

*

⸠[As they ought to be, the Papal Bulls will be superseded by the Holy Scriptures.⸣The veneration of men for the laws of the Papacy, as well as for the opinions of our modern doctors, which since the loosing of Satan they have been at liberty freely to preach to the people, will be restrained within due limits. What concern have the faithful with writings of this sort, except that they are honestly deduced from the fountain of Scripture? By pursuing such a course it is not only in our power to reduce the mandates of Prelates and Popes to their just place, but the errors of these new religious orders also might be corrected and the worship of Christ well purified and elevated.

Men do not now believe sincerely in our Lord Jesus Christ, for if we believed aright in Him, we should acknowledge that *to the Holy Scripture an infinitely greater authority is due* than to any other book. For Christ, our Lawgiver, has given us a law *which in itself is sufficient* for the whole church militant. To be ignorant of the Scripture is the same thing as to be ignorant of Christ. In the Bible the salvation of men is contained.

✻

✻   ✻

✻

[We ought to believe in the authority of no man, unless he say the Word of God. It is impossible that any word or any deed of the Christian should be of equal authority with Holy Scripture.] The right understanding of Holy Scripture is being taught to us by the Holy Ghost just as the Scriptures were opened to the Apostles by Christ. But while Holy Scripture includes in itself all truth, partly mediately, partly immediately, reason is indispensable to the right understanding.

＊
＊　　　＊
＊

The Holy Scripture is the faultless, most true, most perfect, and most holy law of God, which it is the duty of all men to learn, to know, to defend, and to observe, inasmuch as they are bound to serve the Lord in accordance with it, under the promise of an eternal reward.

＊
＊　　　＊
＊

The whole Scripture is *one word of God ;* also the whole Law of Christ is *one perfect word* proceeding from the mouth of God; it is, therefore, not permitted to sever the Holy Scripture, but to allege it in its integrity according to the sense of the author.

If God's Word is the life of the

world, and every word of God is the life of the human soul, how may any Antichrist, for dread of God, take it away from us that be Christian men, and thus suffer the people to die for hunger in heresy and blasphemy of men's laws, that corrupteth and slayeth the soul ?

OF THE SUFFICIENCY
OF HOLY SCRIPTURE.

HE fiend seeketh many ways to mar men in belief and to stop them by saying that no books are belief. For if thou speakest of the Bible, then Antichrist's clerks say, How provest thou that it is Holy Writ more than another written book? Therefore men must use caution, and ask the question whether

Christ left His Gospel here in order to comfort His Church. And if they say that He did, ask them which are these Gospels? These we call Holy Writ. But as Christian men should speak plainly to Antichrist, we say that Holy Writ is commonly taken in three manners. On the first manner Christ Himself is called in the Gospel Holy Writ. On the second manner Holy Writ is called the Truth, and this truth may not fail. On the third manner Holy Writ is the name given to the books that are written and made of ink and parchment. And this speech is not so proper as the first and second. But we take by belief that the second Writ, the truth written in the Book of Life, is Holy Writ, and God says it. This we know by belief, and this our belief makes us certain that these truths are Holy Writ. Thus though Holy Writ on the third manner be burnt or cast in the sea, Holy Writ on the second manner may not fail, as Christ sayeth.

5

ON THE ENGLISH
BIBLE.

S the faith of the Church
is contained in the Scrip-
tures, the more these
are known in their true
meaning, the better; and
inasmuch as secular men should as-
suredly understand the faith they profess, that faith *should be taught to them
in whatever language it may be best
known to them.* Forasmuch also as the
doctrines of our faith are more clearly

and exactly expressed in the Scriptures, than they may probably be by priests;[1] seeing, if I may so speak, that many Prelates are too ignorant of Holy Scripture, while others conceal many parts of it ; and as the verbal instruction of priests have many other defects, the conclusion is abundantly manifest, that believers should ascertain for themselves what are the true matters of their faith, *by having the Scriptures in a language which all may understand.* For the laws made by Prelates are not to be received as matters of faith, nor are we to confide in their public instructions, nor in any of their words, but as they are founded in Holy Writ, since the Scriptures contain (according to St. Austin) the whole truth, and the translation of them into the English language

[1] This doctrine of Wiclif was at the time vehemently opposed by the Romish party. In Walden, one of his bitterest opponents, we read that "the decrees of the bishops in the Church are of greater weight and dignity than the authority of Scripture."

should therefore do at least this good, viz., placing bishops and priests above suspicion as to the parts of it which they profess to explain.

*

*   *

*

Other means (to convert the people), such as Friars, Prelates, the Pope, may all prove defective ; and to provide against this, Christ and His Apostles evangelized the greater portion of the world, *by making known the Scriptures to the people in their own language.* To this end, indeed, did the Holy Spirit endow them with the gift of languages. Why then should not the living disciples of Christ do in this respect as they did in former times ?

ON PREACHING.

HE highest service to which man may attain on earth is to preach the law of God. This duty falls peculiarly to priests, in order that they may produce children of God, and this is the end for which God has wedded the Church. And for this cause Jesus Christ left other works, and occupied himself mostly in preaching, and thus did the Apostles,

and on this account God loved them. But now priests are found in taverns and hunting; and playing at their tables, instead of learning God's law and preaching.

*

*   *

*

The service of preaching is the best having the worst opposed to it. Preaching, if it be well done, is the best of all. Jesus Christ, therefore, when he ascended into heaven, commanded it in particular to all His Apostles to go and preach the Gospel freely to all men. In this stands the office of the spiritual shepherd. As the bishop of the temple hindered Christ, so is He hindered now by the free preaching being prohibited. Therefore Christ told them at the day of doom, Sodom and Gomorrah should better fare than they. Thus, if our bishops and prelates do not preach in their own persons and hinder true priests

from preaching God's law, they are in
the sin of the bishops who killed the
Lord Jesus Christ.

* * *

Prayer is good, but not so good as
preaching; and accordingly, in preaching and also in praying, in the ad-
ministering of the Sacraments, and the
learning of God's law, and the render-
ing of a good example by purity of life,
in these should stand the life of a good
priest.

* * *

In the first law of the Pope it is
stated that each man coming to the
priesthood takes on him the office of a
beadle, to go before doomsday, and to
cry to the people their sins and the
vengeance of God; and since those are
holden heretics who trespass against
the Pope's laws, are not those priests to

be holden heretics who refuse to preach the Gospel, and compel true men to leave the preaching of God's law? All law opposed to their service is opposed to God's law, and to reason and charity, and is for the maintenance of pride and covetousness in Antichrist's laws.

ON THE FREE PREACH-
ING OF GOD'S LAW.

RIARS say plainly that it is apostasy and heresy for a priest to live as Christ ordained a priest to live by the Gospel. For if there be any priest cunning in God's law, and able to travel and to sow God's word among the people; if he do this office freely, going from country to country where he may most profit and cease not, and charge not singular habit, and beg not, but be

paid with common meat and drink, as
Christ and His Apostles were, they will
pursue Him as an apostate, and draw him
to prison, and say that he is cursed for
his deed.   For if this free going about
and free preaching is lawful to such a
friar, since it is exampled and commanded by Christ, and not to be shut
up in a cloister, as it were in Cain's
Castle, so then it should be needed of
friars to cease their living in cloisters
and false obedience, and to dwell
among the people whom they may
most profit spiritually.   For charity
should drive friars to come out amongst
the people, and leave Cain's Castles,
that are so needless and so burdensome
to the people.

ON THE RIGHT OF PRIVATE JUDGMENT.

E are not careful to ex-
plain how it has come to
pass, but manifest it is
that the Church has erred
in this matter (the sole
authority of the Church in spiritual
things) ; and we claim accordingly to
be exempt from its authority in this respect, *and to be left to the guidance of
reason and Scripture.* Surely while it
is permitted to others to choose mere
men as their patrons, it might be permitted to us to choose Him as our
patron who is very God and Man.

ON THE SUPREMACY
OF CIVIL POWER.

HOULD an abbot and all his convent be open traitors, conspiring unto the death of the King and Queen, and of other Lords, and enforce them to destroy all the realm, there may not be taken from them a halfpenny or farthing worth, since all these be temporal goods. Also though other clerks send to our enemies all the rents they have in England, and whatever they may steal from the King's liege men, yet our King may not punish them to a farthing's

worth. Also by the argument of the friars or other clerks, whatever they may be, should they slay Lords' tenants, the King's liege men, and defile Lords' wives, yea the Queen (that God forbid) or the Empress—yet the King may not punish them to the loss of one farthing. Also should they make one of themselves King, no secular Lord may hinder him to conquer all the secular lordships in this earth ; and so they may slay all Lords and Ladies, and their blood and affinity, without any pain in this life, or in body, or in substance. Ye Lords, see and understand with what punishing they deserve to be chastised, who thus unwarily and wrongfully have damned you for heretics. For the chief lordship of all temporalities in the land, both of secular men and religious, pertains to the King of his general governing ; for else he were not King of England, but of a little part thereof.

ON THE RIGHT OF ENGLISH KINGS.

INCE Christ is the chief Lord, and the Pope is a sinner who, according to the theologians, if in mortal sin lacks dominion, and cannot consequently transmit to the English any right to the kingdom, all we need for a true dominion over the realm is to keep ourselves from mortal sin, and give our wealth rightly to the poor, and so hold our kingdom as hitherto immediately from Christ, since he is the chief Lord, giving of Himself full and sufficient authority to all dominion of creature.

ON THE AUTHORITY
OF PARLIAMENT.

 APPEAL to the Church
of the first thousand years
since our Lord's time. I
challenge the existing
Church to dispute these
questions (on the supreme authority of
the Pope) with me. My adversaries
reply that the Church has settled the
matter, and have, in fact, condemned
me beforehand. I cannot expect at
their hands anything else than to be
silenced, and what is more, according
to a new Ordinance, imprisoned. I
know what that means. I demand,
therefore, that the lay voice be heard.

I have appealed to the King against the University ; I now appeal to the King and Parliament against the Synod which is about to use the secular arm —the arm of Parliament. If I am to be tried, let me have a fair trial, and argue my case before the world. If that is not to be, I will at least have care that Parliament shall understand the ecclesiastical points at issue, and the use that is to be made of its power.

That very thing is a mark of the corruption of the Church : but the laity are responsible for its purity. They only conserve the endowments and institutions of the clergy under the condition of that purity. And it has now become a personal matter for them ; it affects their lives and fortunes. If they see their way to clearing off some of its most open corruptions, the English people who have by this time the Bible in their hands, will speedily perceive that I am now no heretic, but the truest Churchman in the land.

OF PCAPAL BULLS.

LL those who falsify the Pope's bulls, or a Bishop's letter, are cursed grievously in all churches four times in the year." Lord, why was not Christ's Gospel put in this sentence by our worldly clerks ? Here it seems to magnify the Pope's bull more than the Gospel ; and in token of this, they punish more the men who trespass against the Pope's bulls, than those who trespass against Christ's Gospel. And hereby men of this world dread more the Pope's lead (seal) and his commandment, than the Gospel of Christ and His commands.

Also a penny clerk, who can neither read nor understand a word of his psalter, nor repeat God's commandments, bringeth forth a bull of lead, witnessing that he is able to govern many souls against God's doom, and open experience of truth; and to procure this false bull, they incur costs and labour, and oftentimes fight, and give much gold out of our land to aliens and enemies. Also the proud priest of Rome getteth images of Peter and Paul, and maketh Christian men believe that all which his bulls speak of is done by authority of Christ; and thus as far as he may, he maketh this bull, which is false, to be Peter's, and Paul's, and Christ's, and in that maketh them false. And by this blasphemy he robbeth Christendom of faith, and good life, and worldly goods.

ON THE GRACE OF GOD.

AITH is a gift of God, and we should therefore know that it may not be given to men except graciously. Thus, indeed, all the good which man have is of God, and accordingly when God rewardeth a good work of man, he crowneth His own gift. This then is also of grace, even as all things are of grace that men have according to the will of God. God's goodness is the first cause why He confers any good to man; and so

it may not be that God doeth good on
men, but if He do it freely, by His own
grace ; and with this understood, we
shall grant that men deserve of God.

*
* *
*

The doctrine of Pelagius and others
who affirm that nothing may be unless
it be of itself, as are mere substances,
is to be scorned and left to idiots.

*
* *
*

Men who love this world, and rest
in the lusts thereof, live as if God had
never spoken in His word, or would
fail to judge them for their doings.
To all Christian men therefore the
faith of Christ's life is needful, and
hence we should know the Gospel, for
it telleth the belief of Christ.

OF PREDESTINATION.

F the Pope asked me whether I were ordained to be saved or predestinate, I would say that I hope so, but I would not swear it nor affirm it without condition though he greatly punished me ; nor deny it nor doubt it, would I no way.

OF FAITH, HOPE, AND CHARITY.

HERE is a faith which is incomplete, as that of devils who believe and tremble ; and another kind of faith is perfect as being inwrought by charity. This charity belongs necessarily to all who are true believers, and all men destitute of it are in a sense unbelievers. The believer is a man who has bestowed upon him by God a faith which is unmixed with doubting. Every man,

therefore, committing sin doeth so as
an unbeliever, for had he been mindful
of the punishment to be inflicted on
the sinner, of the eye of God being
constantly upon him and his doings,
he would not have done so.

⁂
* *
*

Hope is distinguished from faith
in three respects. First, hope has regard only to the attainment of some
future good, but faith has respect to
truth universally, and simply as such.
Secondly, hope falls short of that evidence and knowledge concerning its
object which belong to faith, but rests
half-way between doubt and credulity.
Thirdly, hope has respect only to a
good possible to the person hoping.
Faith, on the contrary, has respect to
things which may be of advantage or
disadvantage to the person who believes,
as well as to things with which he has
no concern at all.

The virtue especially necessary to the Christian pilgrim is charity. Without charity no man can enter heaven. It is the wedding garment, the want of which must bring condemnation at the last judgment. True charity consists in loving God with all the heart, the soul, and the mind; but this command is but poorly observed by our fallen and unhappy race. The second command is like the first : that we love all the works of God, and especially that we love our neighbours as ourselves. The things to which we attend most we love most; now, who is there in our present day who does not think more of that which may bring him money than of that which may fit him for becoming obedient to God's law? But is this to be in charity? Is it not written, " Charity seeketh not her own " ?

Let us see whether the man calling himself a Christian pilgrim is more anxious about his own private advan-

tage than about obedience to the law
of God. When so judged it is plain
that the greater portion of mankind are
wanting in charity ; and if a man be so
rooted in this habit of perverseness,
who can doubt whether that man should
be held a heretic or not ? Who can
doubt to say that not only the laity, but
still more our Prelates, show much
greater concern to guard their private
interests than to uphold the law of
Christ ? How false is the word of such
men when they pretend that they love
God with all their heart ! In truth, all
or the greater part of our religious
orders will fall under condemnation on
the day of the Son of Man. Christ
claimed to have His law observed willingly, freely, that in such obedience
men might find happiness. Hence He
appointed no civil punishment to fall
on transgressors of His commandments,
but left the persons neglecting them to
a suffering more severe, that would
come after the Day of Judgment.

6

OF CONFESSION.

HE confession that is made to man has oft-times been varied in the varying of the Church. For first men confessed to God and to the common people, and this confession was used in the time of the Apostles. Afterwards men were confessed more especially to priests, and made them judges and counsellors of their sinful life. But in the third time since the fiend was

loosed, Pope Innocent ordained a law
of confession that each man of dis-
cretion should once in the year be
privily confessed of his own priest, and
added much to this law that he could
not ground. And although this Pope's
ordinance do much good to many men,
nevertheless many men think that it
harmeth the Church.

ON ABSOLUTION.

 HERE is no greater heresy for a man than to believe that he is absolved from sin if he give money, or because a priest layeth his hand on his head and saith, "I absolve thee;" *for thou must be sorrow-ful in thy heart, else God does not absolve thee.*

OF INDULGENCES.

T is plain to me that our Prelates in granting indulgences do commonly blaspheme the wisdom of God, pretending in their avarice and folly that they understand what they really know not. They chatter on the subject of grace as if it were a thing to be bought and sold like an ass or an ox ; by so doing they learn to make a merchandise of selling par-

dons, the devil having availed himself of an error in the schools to introduce after this manner heresies in morals.

*

*   *

*

I confess that the indulgences of the Pope, if they are what they are pretended to be, are a manifest blasphemy, inasmuch as he claims a power to save men almost without limit, and not only to mitigate the penalties of those who have sinned by granting them the aid of absolutions and indulgences, that they should never come to purgatory, but to give command to the holy angels that, when the soul is separated from the body, they may carry it without delay to its everlasting rest.

ON THE LORD'S SUPPER.

ANY are the errors into which we have fallen with regard to the nature of the Lord's Supper. Some, for example, say that it is a quality without a substance. Others say that it is a nonentity, since it is an aggregate of many qualities which are not all of one genus. Against these opinions I have many a time inveighed, both in the language of the schools and of the common people.

As the words of Holy Scripture tell us that this sacrament *is* the body of Christ, not that it *will be*, or that it is sacramentally a figure of the body of Christ,—so accordingly, we must admit without reserve, on this authority, that the bread which is the sacrament *is* truly the body of Christ. But the simplest layman will see that it follows that, inasmuch as this bread is the body of Christ, it is therefore bread, and remains bread — being *at once* both bread *and* the body of Christ.

*

*　　　*

*

The nature of the bread is not destroyed by what is done by the priest, it is only elevated so as to become a substance more honoured. Do we believe that John the Baptist, when made by the word of Christ to be Elias, ceased to be John?—or ceased to be anything that he was in substance before? In the same manner, the bread while becoming by virtue of Christ's words the body of Christ, does not cease to be bread. 'When it has become *sacramentally* the body of Christ, it remains bread *substantially*.'[1] Further Christ says, " *This is* my body," and these words must be taken as, *i.e.*, in the same sense as, the words referring to the Baptist.

* * * *

If bread consecrated and unconsecrated be mixed together, the heretic cannot tell the difference between the natural bread and his supposed quality without a substance, any more than any of us can distinguish in such case between the bread which has been consecrated and that which has not. Mice, however, have an innate knowledge of the fact. They *know* that the substance of the bread is retained as at first. But our unbelievers have not even such knowledge. They never know what bread or what wine has been consecrated, except as they see it consecrated. *But what, I ask, can be supposed to have moved the Lord Jesus Christ thus to confound and destroy all natural discernment in the senses and minds of the worshippers ?*

*
*   *
*

It is as if the devil had been scheming to this effect saying, If I can by my vicar Antichrist so far seduce the believers in the Church, as to bring them to deny that this sacrament is bread, and to believe it a contemptible quality without a substance, I may after that, and in the same manner, lead them to believe whatever I may wish, inasmuch as the opposite of such a doctrine is plainly taught, both by the language of Scripture, and by the very senses of mankind. Doubtless, after a while these simple-minded believers may be brought to say, that however a prelate may live, be he effeminate, a homicide,

a simonist, or stained with any other
vice, this must never be believed concerning him, by a people who would be
accounted duly obedient. ⌐But, by the
grace of Christ, I will keep clear of the
heresy which teaches that, if the Pope
and Cardinals assert a certain thing to
be the sense of Scripture, therefore so
it is—for that would be to set them up
above the Apostles. ⌐

*
* *
*

Therefore let every man wisely, with
much prayer and great study, and also
with charity read the words of God in
the Holy Scriptures. But many are
like the mother of Zebedee's children,
to whom Christ said, "Thou wottest
not what thou askest." Christ saith, "I
am the true vine." Wherefore do ye
not worship the vine for God, as ye do
the bread?⌐ Wherein was Christ a true
vine? or, wherein was the bread Christ's
body? It was in figurative speech,

which is hidden to the understanding
of the sinners. And thus, as Christ
became not a material nor an earthly
vine, nor a material vine the body of
Christ, so neither is material bread
changed from its substance to the flesh
and blood of Christ. 7

*
* *
*

Should some idiot demand how the
bread may be the body of Christ, and
still remain the same, according to its
own substance and nature—let him
bear in mind his faith in the Incarna-
tion, and see how two different natures
may be united, and still both may not
be the same nature. Would God that
men took heed to the speech of Paul
on this matter, then they would hear
God's word gladly, and despise fables,
and err not in the sacred host, but
grant that it is both things, both bread
and God's body.

*
* *
*

Have you not read that, when Christ
came into the temple, he answered those
asking him, "Cast down this temple
and in three days I will raise it again?"
Which words were fulfilled in his rising
from the dead. But when he said,
"Undo this temple," they were deceived
in that he so meant, for they understood it fleshly, and thought that he
had spoken of the temple of Jerusalem.
But he spake of the temple of His
blessed body, which rose again on the
third day. And just so Christ spake of
His holy body, when he said, "This is
my body, which shall be given for you."
But just as they accuse him falsely
about the temple at Jerusalem, so now-
adays they accuse falsely against Christ,
and say that he spake of the bread
which he brake among the Apostles.
For in that Christ said this *figuratively*,
they are deceived, taking it fleshly,
turning it to the material bread, as the
Jews did in the matter of the temple.

Now, therefore, pray we heartily to

God that this evil time may be made short, for the sake of the chosen men, and that the large and broad way that leadeth to perdition may be stopped, and that the straight and narrow way that leadeth to bliss may be made open by the Holy Scriptures, that we may know what is the will of God, to serve him with truth and holiness. So be it.

OF TRANSUBSTAN-
TIATION.

OF all heresies that have ever sprung up in the Church, I think none was ever more cunningly brought in by hypocrites, or cheats the people in more ways than this; for it robs the people, it makes them commit idolatry, it denieth the faith of Scripture, and in consequence by unbelief provokes the Truth in many ways to anger.

It seems enough for the Christian to believe that *the body of Christ is in a certain spiritual and sacramental manner at every point of the consecrated host,* and that honour should in particular be attributed to that body next after God, and in the third place to that sensible sacrament as to an image or tomb of Christ. [7]

OF THE HEAVENLY
REWARD.

HO would not willingly
suffer in Scotland for the
law and the rights of the
King of England if cer-
tain of returning alive and
unhurt to England, to be rewarded by
the King in proportion to what he had
undergone? Such a man, I say, would
willingly undergo trouble in Scotland,
in the hope of obtaining a reward in
England. Much more, then, should a

man in trouble in this vale of misery manfully strive in faith, hope, and in charity, after the reward of blessedness to be obtained on being translated to his own country.

OF THE MERITS OF SAINTS.

HE Pope and the Friars pretend that there is laid up in heaven an infinite number of supererogatory merits belonging to the Saints, above all the merit of Christ, and that Christ has set the Pope over all this treasure, that he may dispose of it at his pleasure, and distribute therefrom to an infinite extent, since the remainder will still be infinite. All

this is wild blasphemy. Neither the Pope nor the Lord Jesus Christ can grant indulgences to any man except as the Deity has eternally determined by His just counsel. But we are not taught that the Pope or any other man can have any colour of justice to adduce for so doing; therefore the Pope has no such power.

Moreover, it appears that this doctrine is a manifold blasphemy against Christ, inasmuch as the Pope is extolled above His humanity and His deity, and so above all that is called God. For he possesses Cæsarean power above Christ, who had not where to lay His head. In regard to spiritual power it is evident that the Pope is above our Lord Jesus Christ; for it behoved Christ to suffer the most bitter passion for the salvation of man; and we believe that by virtue of Christ's passion men attain to whatever happiness may be theirs. Now the Pope says that it is permitted that he should live as luxuriously as he may choose, and that by the bare writing of one of his scribes, he can introduce wonders without limit into the Militant Church. Who, then, can deny his being extolled above the Lord Jesus Christ, in whose life we do not read that Christ, or any one of His Apostles, granted such absolutions or indulgences?

ON SAINT WORSHIP.

HOEVER entreats a saint should direct his prayer to Christ as God, not to the saint specially, but to Christ. Nor doth the celebration or festival of a saint avail anything, except in so far as it may tend to the magnifying of Christ, inciting us to honour Him, and increasing our love to Him. If there be any celebration in honour of the saints which is not kept within these limits, it is not to be doubted that cupidity or some other evil cause has given rise to

such services. Hence not a few think it would be well for the Church if all festivals of that nature were abolished, and those only retained which stand in immediate relation to Christ. Further they say, the memory of Christ would be kept more freshly in our mind, and the devotions of the common people could not be unduly scattered among the members of Christ. ⌈But, however this may be, it is certain that the service paid to any saint must be useless, except as it incites to the love of Christ, and is of a nature to secure the benefit of His mediation. For as the Scripture assureth us, *Christ is the only mediator between God and man.* Hence many hold that, if prayer were directed only to that middle person of the Trinity for spiritual help, the Church would be more flourishing, and would make greater advances than she now does, when many new intercessors have been found out and introduced.

ON VOWS.

F men foolishly make a vow to go to Rome, or Jerusalem, or Canterbury, or on any other pilgrimage, that we deem of greater weight than the vow made at our christening, to keep God's commandments, to forsake the fiend and all his works. But though men break the highest commandments of God, the rudest parish priest anon shall

absolve him. But of the vows made
of our own heed, though many times
against God's will, no man shall absolve, but some great worldly bishop,
or the most worldly priest of Rome,
the fellow of God and the Deity on
earth.

ON THE SOLDIERSHIP
OF CHRIST.

LL Christians should be soldiers of Christ, and it is plain how many are chargeable with insensibility to this duty, inasmuch as the fear of losing temporal goods and worldly friendships, and apprehensions of the insecurity of life and fortune, prevent so great a number from being faithful either in setting forth the cause of God, in standing

manfully for its defence, or, if need be, suffering death in its behalf. From such a source also comes that subterfuge of Lucifer urged by our modern hypocrites, who say, that to suffer martyrdom cannot be a duty now as it was in the primitive Church, since in our time all men, or at least the great majority, are believers, so that the tyrant is no more who may persecute Christ and his members to the death, and this is the cause why there are not martyrs now as formerly. But it is certain that this excuse has been devised by Satan to shield sin ; for the believer in maintaining the law of Christ should be prepared as his soldier to endure all things at the hands of the proud rulers of the world, so as to declare boldly to the Pope and Cardinals, to Bishops and Prelates, how unjustly they serve God in their offices, inflicting perilous injury on those committed to their care, such as must bring on them a speedy destruction, one way or the other.   All this applies to temporal lords, but not so much as to the clergy ; for as the abomination of desolation begins with a *perverted* clergy, so the consolation begins with a *converted* clergy.   Hence we Christians should declare with constancy the law of Christ even before Cæsarean Prelates, and straightway the flower of martyrdom will be at hand.

ON THE MENDICANT
ORDERS.

N such infinite blasphe-
mies (as granting of abso-
lutions and indulgences
to any extent) the infatu-
ated Church is involved,
especially by the means of the tail of
the dragon, that is, the sects of the
Friars who labour in the cause of these
illusions, and of other Luciferian se-
ductions of the Church. But arise,
soldiers of Christ, be wise to cast away

these things along with the other fictions of the prince of darkness, and put ye on the Lord Jesus Christ, and trust undoubtingly in your own weapons, and sever from the Church such frauds of Antichrist, and teach the people that in Christ alone and in His law they should trust ; that in so doing they may be saved through His goodness, and learn above all things honestly to detect the devices of Antichrist.

ON THE MANNERS
OF FRIARS.

HE Friars become ped-
lars, carrying with them
knives, purses, pens, and
girdles, and spices, and
silk, and precious furs
for women, and thereto small gentle
dogs, to get love of them, and to have
many great gifts for little good or
nought; they covet evil their neighbours' goods.

If they become cake-sellers, giving lords, ladies, and rich men a few pears, apples, or nuts, to have huge gifts to the convent, they will covet their neighbours' goods. They covet unreasonably the houses, that are immoveable goods of their neighbours, like lands or rents, or perpetual alms of coffers, as they bind themselves to the poverty of Christ and His Apostles. And if they lead away men's wives or maidens in their new habits to do lechery as they lust, they break the last commandment. If they make wives and other women their sisters by Letters of Fraternity or other tricks, and get children upon them to make them friars or nuns, to hold up their vain sects by lordship, they covet evil their neighbours' wives and maidens.

So they charge more wrongful commandments of sinful men than the most rightful commandment of God; for if the Pope or a bishop sends a letter for to receive a pardoner who is

to deceive the people by grant of many
thousand years of pardon, he will
always be a help. But if there comes
a true man to preach freely and truly
the Gospel, he will be hindered for
wrongful commandment of a sinful
man. And thus they dread more sinful men than God Almighty. For
when there cometh a pardoner with
stolen bulls and false relics, granting
more years of pardon than come before,
doomsday for the giving of worldly
goods to rich places where there is no
need, he will be assisted and received
by curates in order to have part of
what he gets. But a true priest that
will tell the truth of the Gospel to all
men without glossing and begging from
the poor people will be hindered by
subtle cavillations of man's law.

*

*   *

*

They also teach false chronicles and
fables to colour their worldly life

7 *

thereby, and leave the true Gospel of Jesus Christ. For they love well to tell how their saint lived in gay and costly clothes and worldly array; and so to teach the great penance and sorrow that they did afterwards by which they please God, and not by their worldly life, and then they make people to believe that worldly life of priests, and waste of poor men's goods pleaseth God and is virtuous life.

*

* *

*

See now how Friars do openly against the testament of God. In taking money they do it in many ways; for they lead with them an " Iscariot," stolen from his parents by theft, to rob poor men by begging. They will also count gold and money, and touch it with a stick or with gloves, and a great cup of gold or piece of silver, worth many marks, to drink noble wine, but they will not touch (with the bare hand)

a halfpenny or farthing with the coin
and arms of the cross and of the
King, and this seemeth for contempt of
the cross or of the King, for a wedge
of silver or a cup of gold they will
handle busily, and the money that they
rob of poor men by false begging they
will lay under their bed's head at
night.
    *
  *   *
    *

Friars get commonly both Bishops
and Lords to hinder true preaching, so
that their false preaching be spread,
and thus the people is robbed of all
ghostly and bodily help. They turn
the end of their preaching to get them
such worldly goods; and this intention
must needs make false the manner of
their preaching, for they shape their
sermons more to get them worldly
goods than to benefit the Church
thereby.
    *
  *   *
    *

ON THE LETTERS OF FRATERNITY.

AM willling to say of these Letters in Latin what I have formerly said in English, for it is important to know some-thing of their history. If this be well un-derstood, the simoniacal heresy of those selling them will be immediately mani-fest, for they do not issue such rules except the expectation of realizing gain,

and of giving strength to their unlawful confederacy. Beyond doubt, there is implied in this practice a fraudulent buying and selling ; and it is equally certain that God must hate this hypocritical traffic.

*

*

On many grounds it is evident that the Friars selling these letters have fallen into a radical heresy, for they pretend expressly in them that the individuals to whom they grant them shall be made partakers of merits from themselves after death. But where can you find a more presumptuous blasphemy? For neither they themselves, nor the men with whom they carry on this traffic, can know whether they may not be condemned in hell. How blind, then, is their folly in making assertions on a subject of which they know so little ! But they are, it seems, of such an innate tendency to falsehood, that they do not hesitate to assert, contrary to eternal judgment, that they can do things which in reality they cannot do. Again, if they promise to another man that after death he shall be a partaker of their merits, they manifestly imply, both that the man himself will after death be worthy of such participation, and that they themselves at present merit future happiness; because, if each party should be a foredoomed member of Satan, then such a granting must be beyond the power of these Friars.

*

*　　　*

*

The Friars by the letters which they so assiduously display to the people, give plain indication that they say unto the people that they themselves are holy and grave men in the Church, and, what is more than the ˙sounding of a trumpet before them, they send forth letters to confirm the impression of their sanctity, which men are to preserve constantly in their chests.

Many simple people, however, confide as much in these frivolous letters as in an article of faith like that of the Communion of Saints, or Salvation by Christ. Will, then, a man shrink from acts of licentiousness and fraud, if he believes that soon after, by the aid of a little money bestowed on Friars, an active absolution from the crime he has committed may be obtained? Accordingly this heresy is supposed to be the cause why the faith of the laity is found to be so wavering.

ON THE WORLDLINESS OF THE CLERGY.

MUST tell here how devotion wanteth in clerks, as Popes take their state here for a foul devotion to be worshipped in this world and have much of worldly worship. And so do the Cardinals and the Bishops also. Curates take benefices for the same cause, and priests take their orders for devotion of ten marks (£6 13s. 4d.); religious possessioners for devotion of their belly; and many

Friars take their state to live lustly in this world, for else they should be labourers and live a hard life in a layman's state. And so devotion of clerks, from the first to the last, is study of avarice, and no true devotion; and so Friars, in their states, are wanting right devotion, for they do not take their degrees, neither in school nor in office, for right devotion to run the way that Christ has taught. And they will not be confessors especially of Lords and Ladies for the devotion to make their souls clean, but for devotion of worldly liking that they enjoy with these folks, and of lusts that they have with ladies, other than they should have at home.

ON THE IMMORTALITY
OF THE SOUL.

OBER men entertain no doubt that the soul of man is immortal, and since it is in the soul that we find the identity of the man, it follows that the man must be immortal. For this reason it was that the Apostles of Christ suffered death with such courage and boldness. To them the imprisonment and burden

of the flesh was an irksome restraint
and oppression, and they could therefore rejoice to undergo death for a just
cause. But philosophers assign many
reasons whereby to make good this
opinion. In the first place we are
taught by Aristotle, and in truth by
common experience, that there is a
certain energy in the mind of man that
is imperishable. But no energy or
operation can have more prominence
than is in its subject; now the subject
in this case is the mind or the soul,
the soul therefore must be imperishable. Furthermore we place the human
intellect above all animal faculties.
For in those faculties the brute sur-
passeth man, as the poet sayeth, who
showeth it from experience: "the boar
excelleth us in hearing, the spider in
touch, the vulture in scent, the lynx in
sight, the ape in the sense of tasting."
And since man does not surpass animals
in merely animal sense, we must con-
clude that his excellence lies in his

intellect. But where would be his advantage, if at his death he must part with it. In such case would God not seem to cast contempt on His favoured offspring? Our conclusion, therefore, is that man is possessed of an understanding which he taketh away from the body as a part of his self and which abides for ever. Again, every man has within him the natural desire to live for ever, and the wiser men are, the more they thus feel, and give their testimony to this truth. Now, as nature is not to be frustrated in a purpose of such moment, it is manifest that there is in man, according to nature, a certain understanding that exists for ever—so man is immortal.